for Claire,

always keep reading
and writing!

THE GENIE IN THE BOOK

your
friend,
Cindy Trumbore

For Douglas
–C. T.

Text copyright © 2004 by Cindy Trumbore
Illustrations copyright © 2004 by R. W. Alley
All rights reserved
CIP Data is available

Published in the United States in 2004 by Handprint Books
413 Sixth Avenue
Brooklyn, New York 11215
www.handprintbooks.com

Book design by April M. Ward

First Edition
Printed in China
ISBN: 1-59354-042-6
2 4 6 8 10 9 7 5 3 1

The GENIE in the BOOK

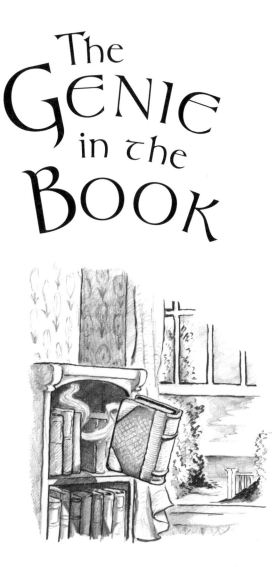

BY Cindy Trumbore

DECORATIONS BY R. W. Alley

Handprint Books 🖐 Brooklyn, New York

Chapter 1

IT SEEMED TO WILL as if his mother had been driving north to Massachusetts forever. They were halfway through Connecticut when Maddy asked, for the millionth time, "Mom, why aren't you and Dad staying with us at Grandma's?"

"We can't leave the diner, honey," Mom said. "If we closed for two weeks now, all our customers might go over to Coffee Island for breakfast and never come back!"

Will spoke up. "You mean you have to keep an

eye on the people at Coffee Island. Dad says they're a bunch of dirty, low-down coffee crooks."

Will's parents owned a diner called Maxine's. It had always been a popular place, but now their town was turning the downtown area where Maxine's was located into a walking mall. Although construction was still going on, a new store had recently opened across from the diner: Coffee Island, part of a big chain.

Will knew that Coffee Island's arrival meant more trouble for Maxine's. Customers already had to dodge around sawhorses, gravel piles, and backhoes just to find the front door. The diner had recently lost two employees, so Will's parents were working nonstop. And now they had seen some of Maxine's customers going to Coffee Island for their morning danish.

"You two will have a great time at Grandma's, even though Dad and I won't be there," Mom said reassuringly.

"I can't wait for my birthday party," Maddy announced. Her birthday was the next day. Grandma had already promised her a party and had invited all the girls Maddy played with when she visited.

Will sighed loudly. He wasn't *sorry* to be going to

Grandma's, but the thought of staying there without his parents seemed strange. Grandma did live right near the beach. It was on the bay, and the warm water and tiny waves were great for swimming. He thought it was possible he might even have a good time at Grandma's, but there were a lot of *ifs*.

He would have fun *if* Grandma didn't get busy with something and leave Will in charge of Maddy and her annoying, horse-crazy friends.

If his cousin Jerome, who lived down the street from Grandma, would stop hatching nutty plans that got them into trouble.

If Grandma took Will, Maddy, and Jerome to one of the beaches on the ocean side of Cape Cod, where there was plenty of surf. Will couldn't wait to try out his new boogie board there.

And *if* he didn't have to worry about Maxine's losing all its customers to Coffee Island. He sighed again.

Mom looked at him in the mirror. She knew about Will's *ifs*. "Don't worry so much, Will," she said. "Who knows? Something wonderful could happen at Grandma's that you don't even know about yet."

That was a typical thing for Will's mother to say.

She always looked on the bright side. She thought every new event was a chance for something nice to happen. Will, on the other hand, liked to test new things out very, very slowly.

Near Providence, Rhode Island, Will started watching for the giant blue bug on the side of the highway. The bug, a huge blue termite that advertised a pest control company, had been there for as long as Will could remember. Sometimes the bug was dressed up for different seasons—a baseball cap and sunglasses for summer, a red nose and reindeer antlers for Christmas.

"There's the sign," Mom said, craning her head. "But where's the bug?"

Will looked. It wasn't there!

"Mom! Why would they take the bug down?" Maddy wailed.

"I don't know. Maybe the pest control company needed to repair it," Mom suggested.

Will was outraged. First he and Maddy had to stay at Grandma's without Mom and Dad. Now the giant blue bug, an important landmark on a long, boring drive, was missing. What else could go wrong?

They found out when they got to Grandma's. From

the outside, everything looked normal. The windows were framed with bright red shutters and window boxes that overflowed with petunias and geraniums. Daylilies lined the driveway. But instead of running out to meet them as she usually did, Grandma just hobbled to the front door, leaning on a crutch. Her right foot was in a cast.

"I broke my ankle. Tripped on a curb," Grandma explained, giving Mom a big hug. "Didn't want to tell you and have you thinking I wasn't up to watching Will and Maddy."

Will's mother started to protest, but Grandma stopped her. "Don't worry. Everything will be fine. I can get down to the beach, no problem. Just can't drive for a while." She winked at Will. "Your Aunt Nancy and Uncle Pete shop for me whenever I need anything. We have plenty of groceries here."

Grandma had a clipped way of talking, and she said *hee-yuh*, as if *here* had two syllables. Usually Will loved to listen to her Massachusetts accent—but not now, when she had such disappointing news.

Maddy said, "You can't drive? So we can't go to the beach with the big waves?"

"Not this trip. Sorry, kids," said Grandma.

Will hugged Grandma hard. She was as soft as a pillow, but her hug back was surprisingly strong. "That's okay about the beach," he said.

"Going to play your clarinet for me, Will?" Grandma asked, standing back and holding him by the shoulders.

"Um, sure," Will muttered without enthusiasm. "At least, I brought it." *What next?* he thought helplessly.

Will's face must have shown his dismay, because Mom wrapped her arm around his waist and hugged him. "Come on, let's go over and say hello to Aunt Nancy and Uncle Pete. I'm dying to see my new niece, and I'm sure Jerome can't wait to see you."

❧

Aunt Nancy let Will hold baby Emily, Jerome's new little sister. She had brown eyes and a mop of red curls, just like Jerome. Will wondered if Emily would have the Look in her eyes someday. The Look was the mischievous expression Jerome had whenever he was cooking up something really bad to do.

"She isn't that much fun yet," Jerome said, "but

she has great toys. Hey, come outside. I've been saving something till you got here."

Will gave the baby to Aunt Nancy and followed Jerome out to the yard. His cousin had set up a launching pad on the grass. A sleek plastic orange-and-yellow rocket sat in the brackets, its nose pointed toward the sky.

"Cool!" Will said. "Did you ever launch one before? Are you allowed to do it by yourself?"

Jerome crouched down by the rocket. "Mom and Dad have been so busy with Emily, I don't think they even remember that I got this for my birthday. Okay, stand back!"

"Shouldn't the brackets be straighter?" Will asked, backing away. Jerome was already touching the starter. The rocket shot up in the air with enormous force. Will watched open-mouthed as it arced toward a second-floor window and zipped through the screen. He heard a terrible crash.

"Jerome!" Aunt Nancy came to the window. "That thing went clear through the screen and broke the flowered ceramic pot! And do you know how close it came to hitting me?"

"Sorry, Mom!" Jerome called cheerfully. "I won't do it again, okay?"

"What flowered ceramic pot?" Will asked.

"The one that holds the toilet brush," Jerome whispered, trying not to laugh. "Mom's in the bathroom!"

"Honestly!" Aunt Nancy said, shaking her head. "Do you know how many times you're going to have to mow the lawn to pay for that screen, Jerome? If Will wasn't here, I'd ground you for the entire week."

"I'm sorry, too, Aunt Nancy," Will said. "Please don't ground Jerome."

"That's all right, Will," his aunt assured him. "I'm sure you had nothing to do with it."

Will was grateful for his aunt's insight. Jerome hated following orders. And because Jerome was a year older, he *especially* wouldn't listen to Will.

Soon it was time for Mom to head home to Commerce, New York. "I want to get back tonight," she explained, and then she kissed everyone good-bye.

After Mom's car pulled away from Aunt Nancy and Uncle Pete's house, Grandma put her arms around Maddy and Will. "Think you can unpack real fast, so you can swim before dinner?" she asked. Maddy and Will nodded and ran back to Grandma's house.

Will grabbed his suitcase and went to his room to unpack. He was pleased that Grandma had put him downstairs this summer, now that he was ten. Last year, he'd been upstairs, sharing a room with Maddy.

He loved this room, with its high ceilings, a window over the bed that showed a glimpse of the ocean, and a big bookcase full of musty old children's books. They had once belonged to Will's mother, who had grown up in this house.

Though he should have been changing into his swim trunks, Will couldn't resist looking at some of the titles in the nearest bookshelf. *Alice's Adventures in Wonderland & Through the Looking-Glass. The Adventures of Tom Sawyer. Little Women. Five Children and It. The Enchanted Castle. Half Magic. The Wind in the Willows. Tales of the Brothers Grimm. The Green Fairy Book. Anne of Green Gables. National Velvet. The Arabian Nights. A Child's Atlas of the World. Treasure Island. The Wizard of Oz. The Lion, the Witch, and the Wardrobe.*

Will closed his eyes, reached out, and picked a book, hoping he wouldn't get *The Green Fairy Book.* He really wasn't in the mood for green fairies.

He put the book on the bed and opened his eyes. He had picked out *The Arabian Nights.* Good!

"Will!" Maddy called. "Are you almost ready?"

"Just a minute. I'm changing!" Will answered. He reached into a drawer and pulled out the swim trunks he'd just unpacked.

Then he flipped the book open. A wonderful old-book smell wafted up from the pages. He had turned to a story called "The Fisherman and the Genie." Will began to read it and was soon caught up in the tale of a humble, aged fisherman who one day hooked a bottle with a powerful genie inside.

He studied the picture of the genie in the book. He was about nine feet tall, with leaf-green skin. He was bald with a little goatee, and he wore a vest, harem pants, and a gold hoop earring. Will thought that, except for the outfit and the green skin, the genie looked very much like the tall policeman who guarded the mall in his town.

Will hardly noticed the knocking at his door. "Will!" Maddy wailed. "It's high tide! Come *on*, or we'll go without you!"

"I'm coming!" Will shouted, wiggling into his suit. "Jeepers, Maddy! Calm *down*! You and Grandma can go on without me. I'll catch up later. I don't like hanging around babies, anyway."

Since she was going to be eight tomorrow, Maddy especially did not like being told that she was a baby. Will was instantly sorry.

He was even sorrier when she yelled back, "Oh, *yeah*? Well, guess WHAT! You're going to be hanging around me at my birthday party tomorrow, because Grandma says *you and Jerome are helping*!" He heard her flounce back down the hall, her flip-flops flapping loudly.

"Oh, no," Will moaned. He fell to his knees helplessly. His head drooped down on the book. "I can't make it through this vacation, I just can't. I need a genius to help me ... I need a genius ... "

At those words, a pale green mist began to rise from the illustration in the book. There was a soft hissing sound, as if someone was filling a helium balloon. Will looked up.

The mist was condensing in a corner of the room. Now it was as tall as the ceiling. It was forming into a green ... person. In fact, it was forming into the exact genie from the illustration in *The Arabian Nights.*

The hissing stopped. The genie put his palms

together and bowed. "Blessings on you, Master," he said. "You asked for a genius. May I grant your heart's truest wish?"

Chapter 2

WILL TRIED not to faint. He stood up, then collapsed on the bed.

"I have offended you, Master?" the genie asked anxiously. He brought his hands together in front of his face and bowed again. When the genie straightened up, his head bumped against the ceiling.

"No, no!" Will said, sitting up. "You haven't offended me. I'm just, um, not used to talking to . . . to . . . Who *are* you, anyway? Oh, man. I'm not really talking to someone who came out of a book, am I?"

"You are indeed, Master," the genie said. "Not a person, but a djinni. A genie, as you would say."

"Okay. Okay." Will tried to wrap his brain around the fact that he'd somehow summoned a genie. He blinked hard, but the genie was still there. He didn't seem fierce, like the one in the story Will had been reading. He was just *huge.*

"How'd you get in that book?" Will asked. "You're so big!"

"Ah, Master," the genie said sadly. "That is a tale. Would you mind if I tell it to you?"

"No problem! Sit down!" Will said.

The genie gracefully sank back until he was sitting on his heels. "Now, to tell my story, I must take you very, very far back in time—three thousand years back. Did you ever hear of King Solomon?"

"Sure, I was just reading about him. He was the king who trapped the genie that the fisherman caught," said Will.

"Ah, you are a bright boy!" the genie said. "Yes, King Solomon had a magic ring that gave him the command of seventy-two djinn. That is the ancient name of my people. The word *genie* comes from the Romans. To a Roman in olden times, I would be called a genius. One genius, two genii."

Will's jaw dropped. "So when I said I needed a genius . . . "

The genie nodded. "Yes, Master. We answer to many names. But to return to my story: We genies built Solomon's beautiful temple in the land of Israel, and we worked in his gold mines. He was not a bad master at first. We got holidays off. But he was very powerful and also very short-tempered. When a genie disobeyed Solomon, or did not please him, Solomon shut him up. Many genies were trapped in brass vessels."

"Like Aladdin's lamp!" Will interrupted.

"Indeed," the genie said. "As the building of his temple went along, the littlest thing would make Solomon angry. He shut up my own wife in a brass jewelry box because she placed a ruby in the wrong wall!"

The genie turned a deeper shade of green. He looked so sad that Will was afraid he might start crying. "I'm sorry," Will said. "How did you end up trapped in a book?"

"Solomon was a great reader," the genie explained. "He happened to have a book in his hand when *I* offended him. He wanted to build the temple doors with cypress wood, and I dared to suggest that he would get a better deal on Lebanon cedar. King Solomon shut me right up in his book."

"That's not fair!" Will said.

"Not a bit," the genie agreed. "But I've found clues in books about the fate of my people. We must grant one hundred people their heart's truest wish before we can be freed. You are my one hundredth master."

"Wow!" Will said. "So once you give me my heart's truest wish, you're free for good? What will you do?"

This time, the genie smiled so broadly that the green mist swirled all the way around the ceiling. "I will find my wife, Master. We will settle down in a green oasis in a desert, and we will live out our days in peace, reading books and serving none but each other."

Will thought about all this. "I don't get it," he said. "How did you get into my mom's old book? It can't be three thousand years old!"

"My first master called me out of Solomon's book," the genie said. "I granted his heart's truest wish, which was to own a fleet of camels for a taxi service. Then I found a newer book to be my next home. It was easy to find pictures of genies in books, for my people have been around since long before humans began to write their stories. And so, Master . . . May I grant your heart's truest wish?"

"Well, wait a minute," Will said. "First of all, you can't keep calling me Master. My name is William Parrish. You can call me Will. What's your name?"

The genie scratched his bald head thoughtfully. "I don't think you could pronounce my name, Master— I mean, Will. Why don't you call me Homer? I'm a book genie, after all, and the *Odyssey* by Homer is my favorite tale. It's about a traveler, and it reminds me a bit of my own travels through this weary world."

"Okay, Homer. Now, do I just get one wish? Because I'm not sure what my heart's truest wish is."

"You get as many wishes as you want, until you gain your heart's truest wish," Homer said. "But don't you know what it is that you want most? Adults always know right away. I never served a child before—perhaps children are more complicated?"

Will nodded. "Sorry about that. I'll have to think about it."

What *did* he want most? For Maddy and Jerome not to drive him nuts? To use his new boogie board?

For Maxine's to have lots of customers again? For the blue bug to come back? For his parents to have a vacation? He really didn't know. He wanted all of those things, but nothing stood out as his heart's truest wish.

Someone pounded on his door. Will nearly fell off the bed. "Are you invisible to other people?" he hissed to Homer.

The genie shook his head. "Quick, call me back into the book!" he said. "Say these words, then clap thrice:

"Spirit of the wind and flame,

Go now, quickly, whence you came."

Will repeated the words and clapped his hands three times. The last bit of green mist was hissing back into the illustration when Maddy burst into the room.

"Why didn't you come swimming with me?" she demanded.

"I got caught up in a story about a genie," Will said truthfully. "Don't drip on the book, okay? And tell Grandma I'm coming swimming now." He realized, as Maddy turned to go back to the beach, that he'd have to start locking his door.

He closed the book and put it under his pillow. Then he grabbed a towel and ran down the pebbled path to the beach, where Grandma waited. The water reflected the late afternoon sun like a golden mirror, and little waves broke in foamy curls by Will's toes.

"Will, I have a favor to ask you," Grandma said. He turned around. Grandma was looking at him apologetically.

"I have to ask you and Jerome to help with Maddy's party tomorrow," she explained, pointing to her cast. "I'll pay you, of course."

Will pretended he didn't already know he was helping with the party. Being paid made it not *quite* so bad. "Okay, Grandma," he said.

All during his swim, Will wondered what he should wish for. He rolled over onto his back and floated for a while with his eyes open. Seagulls squawked as they flapped over the water.

Maddy drifted toward him and pointed upward. "Don't you wish you could fly?" she asked wistfully. "I can fly in my dreams."

Will touched bottom abruptly and stared at his

sister. Suddenly he knew exactly what his first wish was going to be.

⁂

Will set his alarm for 5:30 a.m. When it went off, the sun was just coming up. He could hear gulls calling, already out looking for their breakfast.

After turning the old-fashioned lock on his bedroom door, he quickly pulled off his pajamas and threw on a pair of shorts and his baggy Knicks jersey. Then he reached under his pillow and brought out the copy of *The Arabian Nights*. He flipped to the story about the fisherman and the genie.

There was the picture of Homer. But what, exactly, had he done to call up Homer? Did his head have to be on the picture every time? Maybe it was okay if just some part of his body was touching it.

Will put his hand on the picture and whispered, "I need a genius."

Whoosh! Homer came hissing out of the book. In moments, he was fully assembled in the corner of the room.

He put his hands together and bowed. "Good morning, Will. How may I serve you?"

"Good morning, Homer," Will said. "How are you today?"

"Much the same as I have been for the past three thousand years, thank you very much," Homer replied. "May I grant your heart's truest wish this morning?"

"Well, not yet," Will said. "But could I have an ordinary wish for now? I'd like to have wings, please. I want to fly."

Homer nodded. "I have helped humans to fly before. Let's see . . . what was the first step—creating the wings? Sharing the secrets of aerodynamics?"

Will waited patiently as Homer fingered his gold earring, deep in thought. At one point, Homer scanned the bookshelf and selected *Five Children and It.* As Homer turned the pages quickly, Will remembered that the children in that story flew after *their* magical being, the Psammead, gave them wings.

"I have it," Homer said. "Thank you for waiting, Will. I'm a book genie, as you know. I work by the book."

"What does that mean?" Will asked. "You can only do stuff that you've read about?"

"In a manner of speaking, yes," Homer said. "Of course, I've spent the past three thousand years in some of the finest libraries known to humankind, from the fabled learning centers of ancient Timbuktu to the New York Public Library. There is little I haven't read. Some of my happiest hours have been spent with the *Encyclopedia Britannica*." A dreamy expression flitted over Homer's face, and green mist drifted from his ears.

"Of course, working by the book also means that I can do only one thing at a time. I cannot cut corners, as you would say, and flight is a particularly complicated subject. Think how long it took you humans to figure it out. Now, first: the wings."

Homer put his palms together, thumbs on top, as if he were about to bow to Will. Then he opened them, lifting his palms up as he spread them apart. It looked as if the genie had opened the pages of a book.

Instantly Will felt a pressure on his shoulder blades and understood that these were his new wing bones. He looked over his shoulder, expecting to see white wings. But his wings were gray, and they were much larger than he had expected. He reached back to stroke the long flight feathers with his fingertips. They were soft to his touch, especially at the ends.

Will flexed his wings—a curious feeling, like shrugging his shoulders with a new set of muscles—and knocked the alarm clock off his bedside table. "Oops!" he said. "What am I doing wrong?"

Homer smiled. "I have not yet granted you the secrets of flight. Come, I will take us down to the beach." He closed and opened his palms, and Will gasped. They were standing on the beach. With another motion of his hands, Homer had his own set of wings, with gorgeous green feathers that shimmered in the bright morning sun.

"Ready?" Homer asked. Will nodded. Homer moved his hands one more time. Will instantly knew that if he flapped his wings, he would rise up. He flapped as hard as he could and shot into the air.

"Yikes!" Will fell a few feet, then tried flapping again. This time he had the tempo just right, and he soared over the beach. When he stroked down, his wings tightened up, pushing him forward. When he stroked up, his feathers separated, letting air pass between them.

He practiced gliding on an air current. Homer breezed past him with a smile and a nod.

Flying was the most exciting feeling Will had ever known, better than climbing the hill of a hypercoaster with his eyes closed and then swooping downhill at 100 miles an hour. On a roller coaster, you went only where the tracks led you. Wings took you anywhere you wanted to go.

How far had they gone, anyway? He looked down. The houses below looked like the toy ones in Will's model railroad. His stomach gave a lurch, as if it wanted to turn itself inside-out.

"Homer?" Will called, looking away quickly. "I think I love flying, but I don't like looking down!"

"No problem, Will," Homer said. "I can take away your fear temporarily. Just let me touch down for a moment." Will watched through one eye, his stomach churning, as Homer flew down to the sand and worked his magic with his hands.

"Now try looking down," Homer urged him, returning to Will's side.

Will slowly opened his other eye. The ground didn't frighten him any more. But a lone walker, an elderly woman, was standing on the beach. Her head was tilted as far back as she could get without toppling over.

"How could I forget that we might be seen?" Homer asked. "I believe we are so high up that we just look to the woman like very, very large birds. But if you don't mind, I would like to shrink us down to the size of gulls."

"Why not?" Will said, greedy for more flying. He flew with Homer to the boulders of a jetty, where Homer closed and opened his hands. Instantly the two of them were the size of herring gulls.

Gray and white herring gulls were a constant sight on the beach. One was eyeing the two newcomers on the jetty. It walked stiffly toward the boulders, its neck stretched up and its bill pointed down.

"Is it mad about something?" Will asked. The gull darted to the end of the jetty, still watching Will and Homer, and pulled a mussel out from between two boulders. Then it soared into the air.

"Look out, Will!" Homer called, pushing Will off the rock. Without thinking, Will flapped his wings and rose into the air, just as something came crashing down where he had been standing. It shattered to pieces on the boulder.

"What was *that*?" Will asked.

"It's how the gulls eat their breakfast," Homer said. "They pick off the mussels from the rocks. Then they drop them on the rocks to break them open." The herring gull swooped down, grabbed the soft inner meat of the mussel, and swallowed it with a squeal that sounded like *Yuk-yuk-yuk-yuk*.

"Oh, I get it," Will said. "The gull thought we were moving in on his territory." He flew back and forth over the beach, watching the gulls grab for mussels and spatter them on the rocks. He was idly circling around over the boulders when he felt one wing brush against his, then another. Turning swiftly, he saw an entire flock of gulls barreling toward him. They didn't look friendly.

"Yikes! Homer!" Will yelled, flapping as hard as he could toward Grandma's house. He darted right and left and flew up and down, trying to dodge the angry gulls. *Boof!* Another knocked into him from the side, and Will felt himself falling.

"*Stroke*, Will!" Homer said, flying alongside him.

Will forced his wings to flap down and up, down and up, and he regained his flying altitude. He tried not to look at the gulls all around him. Up close, their bills and claws were razor-sharp. One grazed his leg. Will felt a sting and saw a red streak of blood.

"Keep flying!" Homer called. "I cannot work much magic in the air, but I will slow them down." He closed and opened his palms, and the herring gulls dropped far back. *Gah, gah, gah!* they called mockingly.

Soon Will and Homer were flying over Grandma's backyard. Will adjusted his wings and landed next to the garden. Homer dropped down next to him. "Quick, Homer! Change us back!" Will panted.

Homer clapped his palms together, then raised and opened them. Will was his normal size again. Next to him, Homer was nine feet tall once more. He was quite a sight with his enormous green wings. Will hoped Grandma and Maddy were still asleep.

Will looked up and saw the startled herring gulls stop and hover overhead. *Yuk-yuk-yuk-yuk!* they cackled. Then they flew back to the beach.

Homer's hands moved again, and the two sets of wings vanished. Then they were once more standing in Will's room.

At the sight of his bed, Will gave an enormous yawn.

"Thanks, Homer! Wow, am I tired." He couldn't wait to climb back into bed, but he forced himself to think about Maddy's party.

"I'm going to need you again this afternoon," he said. "It's still not my heart's truest wish, but you'd really come in handy at Maddy's birthday party. Jerome and I have to help Grandma. Could you keep the girls out of our hair? Entertain them, maybe?"

"I am at your service, Will," Homer replied. He nodded thoughtfully as Will described Maddy and her friends. "I know what young girls enjoyed when I was a young djinni, in ages past," he said. "They liked horses then, too. Why don't I do a little research in your fine library this morning while you sleep? I'd like to catch up on young people of the past few centuries."

"Sure. Read away," Will said. Covering another yawn, he got into bed. He could tell that the genie was just itching to get his hands on the books on the shelf. A pale green mist was already reaching toward *Treasure Island*.

Will could hear Grandma's crutch as she limped down the hall toward the kitchen to start the coffee maker. Then he fell into a deep, dreamless sleep.

Chapter 3

WILL WOKE UP again at nine to find Homer kneeling by the bookshelf, deep into his mom's old copy of *National Velvet*.

"Hi, Homer. Have you figured out what to do at Maddy's party yet?" he asked.

"I believe so, Will," Homer said. "You may call me back into my book now."

Will fished *The Arabian Nights* out from beneath his pillow.

"Spirit of the wind and flame,

Go now, quickly, whence you came,"

he chanted, clapping his hands three times.

Homer dissolved into a green mist that hissed back into the genie picture.

At the breakfast table, Maddy was showing Grandma the place cards she had made for her four party guests. "What will we do at my party, Grandma?" she asked.

"You'll have lemonade and cookies, " Grandma said. "And then games."

"Ooh! What sort of games?" Maddy asked, spearing one of Grandma's delicious pancakes.

"Hide-and-seek. Hopscotch. Got lots of chalk so you can draw on the driveway." Grandma waved her hands. "You and Jerome won't have much to do, Will. Little girls entertain themselves. Oh, and Maddy, I told each girl to bring her favorite stuffed animal."

Maddy sighed with pleasure. "They'll *all* bring horses, of course," she said. Will just kept chewing steadily. He would need proper nutrition to face the day ahead.

<hr>

Jerome arrived at 1:30. He clutched his throat and

pretended to throw up as soon as he saw the table with its five little chairs.

They set the table with the plastic tea service that Grandma had bought just for the party. There was a teakettle, sugar bowl, cups and saucers, little plates, and a large tray, all decorated with horses and a lot of pink hearts.

Will poured lemonade into the kettle while Jerome meekly filled up the bowl with lumps of sugar. In the kitchen, Grandma lined the tray with doilies and piled it high with her homemade brownies and sugar cookies.

They were all ready when the girls arrived. Each one was carrying a stuffed horse, and Maddy squealed as she greeted each girl. "*Kelly!* Oh, you brought Cuddles. And *Lauren.* I'm so glad you brought Midnight. Look, I have Shadow. *Amanda! Amelia!* What are your horses' names?"

Will couldn't tell the Fuller twins, Amanda and Amelia, apart. It figured that they had identical horses called Starfire and Wildfire. He looked at Jerome out of the corner of his eye. Jerome was pretending to saw a plastic knife across his neck.

"Sit down, girls!" Grandma said. "Help yourselves to

lemonade—I mean, lemon tea—and some goodies."

The girls sat in the little chairs and began chattering away about their horses. Will and Jerome grabbed a couple of brownies and cookies. They stretched out under a tree, away from the girls, and Jerome told Will about a new trading-card game that everyone was playing at his school.

The phone rang inside the house. "Will, please answer the phone for me, dear," Grandma called. "Tell whoever it is that I'll be there soon."

Will ran for the phone and picked it up on the third ring. "Hello?" he said.

"Will?" It was Mom.

"Mom! Wow! How are you?" he asked. "How's Dad? Is he there? Can I talk to him?"

"Oh, honey," his mother said. "Not right now, okay? The Sunday brunch crowd is gone, and Dad is cleaning up. But he'll call you tonight, for sure. Are you having a good time? How's Maddy doing?"

Will told her all about the birthday party. By the time he was done, Grandma had appeared at the door. He said good-bye to his mother and handed the phone to Grandma.

Grandma had set up a chair by the phone, with a stool next to it where she could rest her cast. She sank down with her back to the yard and put her foot up. "Maxine?" she said. "How are you, dear?"

Will could tell by the way Grandma's face changed that whatever Mom was saying wasn't good. Then Grandma said, "Coffee Island did *what*? Slow down, dear, you're speaking too quickly."

Will frowned. Grandma covered the phone. "Will, dear, please go check on the tea party. I'll be there as soon as I can."

He went out to the yard to find utter chaos. The girls were throwing sugar lumps into the air for their horses to catch. Since the horses were stuffed, the girls had to catch the lumps for them—in their mouths. They seemed to get wilder with every sugar lump they ate.

One of the twins said, "Let's find a real horse!" They all ran toward Jerome, who jumped to his feet and began edging away. Amanda-or-Amelia hopped on his back and kicked her heels into his sides. "Giddyup, horsie!" she shouted.

Jerome saw Will. *"Help!"* he yelled.

It was time for Homer, no doubt about it. "Be right

back!" Will shouted and ran into the house.

Grandma was still talking to Mom. When she wasn't looking, Will edged behind her and pulled down the shade on the window that faced the yard. Then he raced to his room, grabbed *The Arabian Nights*, and rushed toward the backyard.

Poor Jerome now had Maddy on his back. "Will . . . Will . . . " he panted. "Can't hold out much longer. Help me . . . help me . . ."

Will ducked behind the nearest tree and quickly flipped through the pages of *The Arabian Nights* to the picture of Homer. Touching it, he said, "I need a genius!"

In moments, Homer was bowing in front of him. "Yes, Will? What can I do for you?"

Will stabbed his finger in the direction of Jerome. "Help him out! *Now!*"

"Ah!" Homer said happily. "You want the entertainment!" He put his palms together, then opened them and lifted them up as if he were opening a book. Maddy slipped off Jerome's back.

"Hey!" she said. "Where'd my horsie go?"

Homer turned in the direction of Maddy's stuffed horse, Shadow, and touched his hands together again.

Instantly the horse began to grow . . . and grow . . . and grow.

The five girls fell silent as the horse changed from stuffing to bones, from cloth to skin. When it stood at about sixteen hands, it whickered softly.

"Shadow!" Maddy exclaimed. "You're *real*!"

She ran to stroke the horse's neck. Then she turned to Homer and said, "Thank you! Hey, are you the policeman from the mall? What are you doing here?" She didn't wait for an answer, but turned back to Shadow. Will remembered all over again how much Homer resembled the policeman at the mall at home. He guessed Maddy hadn't noticed Homer's green skin, or that he was nine feet tall and had suddenly appeared from behind a tree. Horses drove all sensible thoughts from Maddy's mind.

Jerome said, "Will? Could you tell me what's going on here?"

Will pointed to the book, then to Homer. "He's a genie," he answered. "A book genie. I called him, and he came."

Jerome nodded. "Okay." He sat down on the ground suddenly.

"Mr. Policeman! Mr. Policeman!" the other girls shouted. "Can you make our horses real, too?"

Homer looked at Will, who nodded. "Surely," the genie said. One by one, he enchanted each girl's stuffed horse until it was the right size for each girl to ride. He outfitted the horses with saddles and bridles, and the girls with riding gear and helmets. And he kindly linked his hands together to give each girl a leg up onto her horse.

Five horses took up a lot of room in one backyard and were awfully restless, too. They were stamping their feet and prancing in circles.

"Could you give the girls some instant riding lessons, and maybe a trail to follow?" Will asked.

"Indeed!" Homer said cheerily. "I know just the thing." He closed and opened his palms, and each girl sat up straighter on her horse.

But it was Homer's next creation that really got Will's attention. This time, when he opened up his hands, an entire racecourse appeared.

Behind Grandma's yard was a stretch of scrubby pine trees, so dense that no kid ever set foot in there. Suddenly, the pine trees were gone. The track that replaced them looked a mile long. Along the way, jumps were set up, ranging in height from four to six feet. Open ditches stretched in front of several jumps. One jump had a ditch on one side and a babbling brook on the other.

Will opened and closed his mouth, trying to make sounds come out. He'd read about a course like this before, but where?

He remembered. "The Grand National!" he said. "It's a steeplechase race, like in *National Velvet.*" In the Grand National, each horse made thirty jumps during the course of the race, and some of the jumps—called fences—were extremely difficult. To get over the ditches and brook, the horses had to make jumps that weren't just high, but long.

"Yes, Will," Homer said proudly. "But not the real National—a scale model. There are half as many jumps, and the course is half as long."

Homer had conveniently put a starting place for each horse at the beginning of the course, and the five horses were lining up. They were wearing silk riding colors, Will noticed.

Jerome staggered to his feet. "Hey! Wait a minute,

genie!" he called out. "I'm Will's cousin, Jerome. Sorry, I don't know your name—"

"Homer," the genie said politely.

"Okay, Homer. Do they"—he pointed to the girls, whose horses were frisking in the stalls—"know how to jump?"

"Certainly," Homer said. "I gave them the experience of the most famous jockeys ever to race in the Grand National."

An announcer's voice came over an invisible P.A. system: "And they're off! . . . Out of the post, it's Wildfire, making a strong start as she heads for the first turn. Close on Wildfire's heels is her twin, Starfire. Coming up on the inside it's Shadow, followed by Cuddles and Midnight. Shadow is a strong favorite in today's race, despite the fact that only two grays have ever won the Grand National. . . ."

Will couldn't believe his eyes or ears. The horses had reached the first jump. They sailed over it, one by one, and began running furiously toward the second jump—one with a ditch in front of it.

Jerome was watching the race through his fingers.

"But, Homer," he asked, "can't even the best jockeys *fall down*?"

"Of course they can, Jerome," Homer said. He turned to Will, looking puzzled. "Wasn't a racecourse a good activity for Maddy's party? I read about this one in *National Velvet,* and it sounded like just the thing!"

"Well—" Will paused, wondering if he could be dreaming.

"Shadow is passing Starfire . . . he's passing Wildfire . . . he's taken the lead, ladies and gentlemen!" the announcer said. "Shadow is in the lead, heading for the second fence. It's the first open ditch, a trench of six feet. If the horse judges this one poorly, it could be the end of the race for Shadow and his rider, Maddy Parrish."

Will watched as Maddy's horse tensed, getting ready to jump. This was not a dream. He didn't even *know* enough about racing to dream all this stuff. "Homer!" he shouted. *"Stop the race now!"*

"Certainly, Will," Homer said. He quickly closed and opened his palms, just as Maddy's horse drew his legs under him for the jump. Shadow froze in midair over the fence. Will looked around. The other horses had frozen, too. The girls, however, had not.

"Aw!" he heard Maddy complain. "What happened? Go, Shadow!" She kicked the horse lightly with her boots, but it stayed frozen in the air. Then she looked at the ground and shrieked, "Get me doooooown!" The other girls were starting to wail.

"Hurry, Homer," Will said.

"I'm a book genie, Will," Homer reminded him gently. "I will do my best to hurry, but that is not the way I work." He closed and opened his hands. Shadow floated down to the ground and began to shrink. The same thing happened to the other horses, until they all turned back into stuffed animals. The girls' riding outfits disappeared, and the fences and ditches melted away. In their places, the scrubby pine trees began to spring up.

Homer paused, his green forehead wrinkling in thought, before touching his hands together again. Each girl and her stuffed horse disappeared in a shower of green sparks.

Will couldn't see anything but pine trees now. "Where—?" he yelled. He heard a sound behind him and turned around. The girls had reappeared around the table.

"*I* was winning," Maddy announced. The girls all started arguing at once.

"Make them forget it ever happened, please, Homer," Will said.

Homer looked disappointed, but he nodded.

"I want to remember, though," Jerome said quickly.

Will considered this. Jerome *had* been concerned about the girls' safety. What if he hadn't asked Homer if the girls could fall off their horses?

"Okay, Jerome can remember," Will said. Jerome gave him two thumbs-up.

Homer touched his palms together one last time, and the girls stopped quarreling. Amelia-or-Amanda picked up her horse. "Let's have a pretend race!" she said.

"That's a great idea!" Will said. "Now it's time to say good-bye to Mr. Policeman here."

The girls were on their hands and knees in the grass, playing with their horses. They barely looked up as Will led Homer over behind a tree.

"Will, I believe I require a day or so to rest," Homer said, looking very serious. "Creating the racecourse was not difficult, as I had just read about it in *National Velvet*. But clearing away the girls' memories was not so easy for me. My experience is with adults, and they do not generally want anyone to forget the wishes I have granted."

"That's all right, Homer," Will said. "That will give me more time to think about my heart's truest wish, anyway."

"Ah," Homer said, nodding and bowing. Will bowed in return and said the spell to send Homer back into the book.

"How's it going, kids?" Grandma called from the front door.

Maddy smiled angelically. "Grandma, we're having a horse race," she said.

"Wonderful!" Grandma said. "Boys, you're doing a splendid job. Isn't it just as I said? Little girls entertain themselves."

After the party, Will and Jerome walked down to the beach by themselves. "I'll come along soon," Grandma said as she waved them off. "Don't swim till I get there."

The boys started down the path, the pebbles crunching under their water shoes. Tangles of beach plum, the fruit still green, shot every which way on either side of the path. Dragonflies launched themselves from tall Queen Anne's lace, and spiky sea holly waved in the wind.

"So, you saw Homer," Will told Jerome. "Like I said, he's a book genie. He can do anything as long as he's read about it. He'll grant me as many wishes as I need, until I decide on my heart's truest wish."

"You don't know what you want?" Jerome asked.

"No. I want a lot of things, but when I really think about it, none of them stands out." He told Jerome about his flying adventure. "It got a little weird when the seagulls tried to attack us, but it was still awesome. It wasn't my heart's truest wish, though."

They reached the edge of the water. Jerome ran in and didn't stop until he was waist-deep.

"Grandma doesn't want us going in alone," Will reminded him. He followed till he was just up to his knees in the warm water.

"I'm not really *going in*," Jerome said. He went in a

little further, till the water came up to his chest. "See? I'm not swimming yet, so I'm not going in." Will just sighed.

"What are you going to ask Homer for next?" Jerome asked.

"He needs a day off," Will explained. "So I can't ask him right away. But I really want to find a beach where I can use my new boogie board."

Jerome gasped. "Can I come?" He held his hands up like begging doggy paws. "Please, please, please?"

Will had to laugh. "Yes, but I would have included you anyway."

Grandma came into sight, hobbling down the path with Maddy at her side. *"Jerome! You wait to swim till I can see you!"* she hollered.

After that, the two boys just had fun in the water the way they always did at Grandma's—swimming, splashing each other, doing underwater handstands and dead man's floats—as if the wild party had never happened at all.

Chapter 4

LATER THAT EVENING, Will's father called.

After telling him a very edited version of the party, Will couldn't help asking, "Dad? When Mom called Grandma this afternoon, what did she say about Coffee Island?"

Dad said that Coffee Island was offering the same breakfast special that Maxine's offered every morning—coffee and a danish—but for fifty cents less than Maxine's charged. "It certainly looks like they're trying to put us out of business," Dad said. "But don't worry, Will. We have loyal customers, and we'll come out of this just fine."

"I guess," Will said. The whole problem made his head hurt.

He went to his room and leafed through the *Child's Atlas of the World*. The oversized book was old and musty, and the people in the pictures had old-fashioned clothes, but Will figured geography probably hadn't changed too much since his mother was a kid.

In the section on Australia, a photo caught his eye. It showed a surfer riding a monster wave, and the caption underneath said, QUEENSLAND, AUSTRALIA: SURFER'S PARADISE.

"Bingo!" Will said. Queensland, it turned out, had year-round swimming. Just off the coast was the Great Barrier Reef, home to thousands of kinds of fish. He and Jerome could boogie board for a while, then visit the reef, maybe snorkel a little. Will noted that when it was midnight in Massachusetts, it was afternoon in Queensland. They could leave for their adventure at midnight, and nobody would ever know!

He wandered out to the living room, where Grandma was playing Go Fish with Maddy. "Is it okay if Jerome sleeps over tomorrow night?" he asked.

"Sure, dear," Grandma said. Will congratulated

himself on the brilliance of his plan. Everything was going ... well ... swimmingly.

⁓〇⁓

Will and Jerome went exploring on their bikes the next day. It was sunny but not too hot, and they rode around for hours. Will's idea of exploring was to ride down streets that had interesting names, such as Dead Man's Way. Jerome's was to look for roads with signs that said PRIVATE BEACH—NO TRESPASSING, then ride to the private beaches and back as fast as possible. "See, it's not trespassing unless you hang around," Jerome said with the Look in his eye. They never were caught, but Will kept watching over his shoulder the entire time.

Both boys were glad to go to bed early that night. They were sound asleep when Will's bedside alarm clock *beep-beep-beep*ed at midnight.

Will fumbled under his pillow for *The Arabian Nights.* He opened the book and put his hand on the picture of Homer. "I need a genius," he said, trying not to yawn.

Whoosh! Homer materialized in the middle of the

room. Will immediately felt more awake. In his sleeping bag on the floor, Jerome sat up quickly.

"Have you thought of your heart's truest wish, Will?" Homer asked, putting his hands together and bowing. "And may I thank you for that delightful rest?"

"You're welcome," Will said. "I still don't know my heart's truest wish, but I thought of someplace fun to go." He showed Homer the atlas.

Homer quickly scanned the article. He nodded. "It will be my pleasure to transport you to Queensland, Will. I've read many articles about Australia in *National Geographic.* But perhaps you boys could change into your swimsuits first."

"My swim trunks are in the upstairs bathroom," Jerome said. "I'll be right back. Don't go without me!"

Will had just pulled a T-shirt over his swim trunks when he heard a knock on the door.

"Come in," he called. The door opened, and Jerome walked in, followed by Maddy.

"What are you guys up to?" Maddy demanded. "First Jerome comes banging around the upstairs bathroom and wakes me up. Then he comes out in his *swimsuit!*"

"Shhhhh!" Will put his hand around her mouth. "Maddy, if you breathe one more WORD, we'll wake up Grandma, and then what do you think will happen?"

"'I 'on't 'ow. 'At?" Maddy said. "'Et 'o of 'e!"

"What?" Will asked, taking his hand away.

"I said, 'Let go of me,'" Maddy replied in an angry whisper.

"But you'll ruin *everything*," Will said, taking his hand away. "Now, run back to bed, like a good little girl."

"No." Maddy crossed her arms. "What are you going to do? Swim at night? Grandma wouldn't like it. It's not safe, and I'll tell."

She noticed Homer. "Oh, hi," she said, sounding confused. "Aren't you the policeman from the mall?"

"This is Homer," Will said. "Actually, you met before. You just don't remember."

"Hello, Maddy." Homer gave his usual bow. "How pleasant to see you again."

"Anyway, we're *not* swimming at night," Will said. "We're going someplace . . . it's hard to explain . . . but someplace where the sun is shining. And Homer's going to watch us. He's a grown-up. Maddy, I don't have time to tell you everything, but I really need you to go back to bed now."

"I'm not going." Maddy stared up at Will. "Either you take me with you, or I yell for Grandma." She stamped her foot. "Right now!"

Will slumped down till his head touched his bed. "I give up," he said. "All right! You can come!" He turned to Homer. "Could you give her an instant swimsuit? Please?"

"Certainly, Will," Homer replied cheerily. He touched his palms together and opened them upward. Maddy was now wearing a white tank suit with little pink ruffles.

"Let's get to the beach in Queensland, Homer!" Will said. "Before Grandma wakes up."

"Indeed." Homer moved his hands again, and then the room disappeared in a swirling mist. In moments, Will, Jerome, Maddy, and Homer had been transported to the shore of a beautiful beach.

Waves crashed on the sandy shore. A handful of surfers were paddling out on boards to catch the curling, perfectly rideable waves.

Homer's hands moved so quickly they were a blur.

First, four striped beach towels appeared on the white sand. Overhead stretched a large, drooping beach umbrella, big enough to hide Homer's unusual height and green skin from onlookers. Homer ducked under the umbrella and covered himself from head to toe in another oversized striped towel.

From underneath the towel, Homer was still working his magic. Three boogie boards, a bottle of sunblock, and a ten-pack of cold juice boxes appeared in the sand next to the towels.

"Wow!" Maddy said. "How did Homer do all that?"

"He's a book genie," Will explained. "I summoned him out of an old book. He'll keep granting my wishes until I decide on my heart's truest wish." Maddy nodded, open-mouthed.

Will picked up the nearest boogie board. "Homer, you're not going in with us?"

Homer shook his head. "We djinn don't care to swim. Perhaps it is because we are part-fire."

The three kids rode one incredible wave after another. After an hour, they flopped in exhaustion on their striped towels.

Will popped a straw into a juice box and took a long

drink. He'd set his waterproof watch for Queensland time, and it read 4:20 p.m. "Let's visit the Great Barrier Reef!" he said.

"Surely, Will," Homer replied, sitting up from his towel. "How would you like to visit the reef?"

"What are my options?" Will asked.

"I could give you all some snorkeling gear and instant lessons, and you could float around looking at fish. I would watch you from one of the islands in the reef. Or . . . I could turn us all into fish, and we could observe the beauties of the Great Barrier Reef firsthand."

Will sat up. "Really?"

"Well, we djinn are shape-shifters. If I turned us into fish, we wouldn't need snorkeling gear or lessons." Homer's expression reminded Will a bit of Jerome's puppy-dog look. "I haven't shape-shifted in years, and I must confess that I long to try it again."

"I want to be a fish!" Maddy said.

"You wouldn't mind getting wet, Homer?" Will asked, just checking.

"Not as a fish, no. Just as a genie."

Will cocked an eyebrow at Jerome. "What about sharks and stuff?" Jerome asked.

Homer nodded thoughtfully. "Good point. I'll take us to a part of the reef that has no sharks."

Will grinned. "Okay, Homer. Please turn us into fish on the Great Barrier Reef!"

Afterward, Will wondered if the people on the beach around them had been puzzled by their sudden disappearance. As soon as Homer opened his cupped palms, Will found himself underwater, swimming over a stretch of deep blue coral.

"Wow!" he said, watching bubbles come out of his mouth. He looked through the clear water and saw a jellyfish drift by, propelled by the current.

He tried saying "hi!" to the jellyfish, but only bubbles came out of his mouth. The jellyfish gave him a puzzled look.

Over here, Will! he heard. The words had formed, one by one, inside his head. He turned to see three fish swimming near him. Were they Homer, Maddy, and Jerome? He couldn't tell. One of the fish was waving its long top fin at him.

It's Homer! That's me, waving! said the voice inside Will's head.

Could he *think* a message back to Homer? He decided to try.

What are we, Homer? And who's who? he asked, concentrating on the waving fish and thinking the message as forcefully as he could.

You are a parrotfish. Homer's words appeared in Will's mind. *See that rainbow-colored fish with the large beak over there? You look just like that.*

Homer waved his long top fin again. *I'm an angelfish,* Homer continued. He had a white body with black stripes.

What are Jerome and Maddy? asked Will.

Maddy is the golden damselfish swimming above that staghorn coral over there, Homer told him. Will saw a little yellow fish hovering over a head of coral that had branches, like a deer's antlers. *Damselfish are small, but brave,* Homer added.

Will spotted some algae on the coral. He darted over to scrape it off and eat it with his beaklike mouth. It tasted delicious, like licking the spoon after Mom made fudge.

And Jerome is passing you on your left, the voice continued. Will saw a bright orange-and-yellow fish flash by. It darted into an anemone to hide. *Jerome is—*

Homer gave a little cough, or perhaps he was hiding a chuckle—*a tomato clown fish.*

Will laughed silently. A manta ray passed him, flapping its long, flat fins.

Whoa, look at that! Jerome said, swimming out of the anemone. He pointed to something that looked clam-like, only it was about a million times bigger than a normal clam.

Don't get too close to the giant clam, Homer called.

Why not? Jerome swam right up to the open shell and looked in. The shell began closing slowly around him.

Look out! Will yelled.

Jerome darted out as the shell's two halves clamped shut. *Hey, Homer!* he said. *What would we see farther out in the water?*

Oh, we shouldn't go out there, Homer said.

It's okay. Your magic can protect us! And with that, Jerome turned and swam away from the shallow waters of the reef toward the deeper water.

Come back here, Jerome! Will yelled. He, Homer, and Maddy swam as fast as they could after the clown fish's rapidly disappearing tail.

Clown fish are playful, Homer said apologetically. *That's why I turned Jerome into one. It's all my fault.*

It's all JEROME'S fault, Will said. *He just can't stand being told he can't do something!*

What's out there, Homer? Maddy asked.

We're moving toward the waters where the fishing boats come in, Homer said. The biggest fish Will had ever seen swam by.

Barramundi cod, Homer said. *A very popular fish— on Australian menus.*

Will began to feel afraid. *Should you use your magic, Homer?* he asked.

I will, Homer said. *It will take me a minute or two to get us back to shore and undo our shape-shifting. You know, I'm a—*

Book genie, Will said, finishing his sentence. *You do things by the book. I know, Homer, but please, hurry!*

Suddenly they heard Jerome call, *Homer! Help! I'm caught in a net!*

Now they could see a large net stretching ahead of them. Jerome was tangled in the white mesh.

Homer darted forward. He tried to use his long, graceful top fin to free Jerome from the net, but it was useless. After a few tries, Homer was caught as well.

Swim away, Will! Homer said. *Protect Maddy! I'll find a way to save Jerome.*

Will nudged the little damselfish that was Maddy, and they swam away. They were going against the current now, and it was hard to swim.

Suddenly Will saw a huge fish with sharp teeth bearing down on them hungrily. *Oh, no!* he yelled. *Use your magic, Homer!*

I can't use it now! I need to touch my fins together! Homer called.

The giant fish was heading straight for Will. To his amazement, Maddy zipped around until she was chasing the big fish. She darted forward and bit its tail. The fish tried to shake her off, but Maddy bit it again and again.

With a flap of its tail, the big fish swam away. As it disappeared from sight, the white mesh of the net began to move toward Will and Maddy, bundling them together with several fish swimming nearby. Then it began to haul all the fish—Will, Maddy, Jerome, Homer, and the others—up out of the water.

The net rose above the surface of the water. Will

could see sunshine, and he began to gasp. The phrase "like a fish out of water" came to his mind. It never meant anything good.

The net full of flopping fish hit the deck of a boat. *Ouch!* Will yelled. He wished with all his heart that they had stayed home at Grandma's. Wasn't it enough to be near the ocean? Who needed boogie boarding, too? He promised himself that if they got out of this alive, he'd try to find an adventure closer to home.

The fishermen were talking to each other. "Look, mate!" one said to the other. "What's that sail out there to the west?"

The other one peered west, toward the afternoon sun. "Coming awfully fast," he said. "Only one sailor. Odd." He shrugged and reached for the net. Will flopped around inside it, trying to see over the edge of the fishing boat.

A little boat with one large sail was approaching the fishing vessel, expertly steered by a tall, dark-skinned man who wore a brightly patterned tunic and pants and a white turban. The turbaned sailor reached the fishing boat, tied his boat up alongside, and hopped aboard.

"Sinbad the Sailor has answered the call of his

friend, the mighty djinni," the man declared in a thundering voice. "What do you mean, trapping my friends in your paltry fishing net?"

"Sinbad?" asked one of the sailors, scratching his head. "I don't think I heard you right, mate. That's a bloke in a movie, or something." He dipped a bucket in the ocean and threw the water over the captive fish, much to Will's relief.

"I am Sinbad, champion of the seas!" said the man in the turban. He clapped his hand over the jeweled scabbard that hung from his sash. "I'm the hero of seven voyages, and friend to kings and poor men alike!"

Will remembered from *The Arabian Nights* that Sinbad was rather boastful. He wished the sailor would get his bragging over with and hurry up and rescue them.

"Friend to the poor man? Then you're our friend, Sinbad! And which of your mates have we trapped here?" asked the other fisherman, giving his friend a wink.

Sinbad pointed to the net. "My genie friend is in there, with several youngsters who are entrusted to his care. Release them immediately, or I shall draw my mighty sword!"

"Aw, don't do that, mate," said the first fisherman. "You might hurt somebody. And our dinner's inside that net. What will you give us in return?"

Sinbad reached into the pouch that hung from his sash and pulled out two diamonds. "I will give you each a priceless gem from the Valley of the Diamonds. The valley was filled with monstrous serpents, which I escaped only by using the greatest cunning and wit."

"They're pretty." The second fisherman said, turning the diamond over in his grimy hand. "Are they real?"

"*Real?*" Sinbad drew a long, sharp-looking sword from his scabbard. "You doubt the word of Sinbad the Sailor?"

Sinbad, not now! Will heard Homer call. *We need your help! I'm the angelfish in the net, and my young friends are the clown fish, damselfish, and parrotfish. The sailors have no need of us, yet they keep us against our will.*

Sinbad put his sword away, shaking his head sadly. "Yes, the diamonds are real, you shore-hugging nincompoops! And now, may I have your catch?"

"Sure, Sinbad. Here you go." The first fisherman handed over the net full of fish. Sinbad took it lightly and hopped into his boat, where he plunged the net into the water. Will had thought flying was the greatest feeling in the world, but he decided he'd been wrong. Cool water washing all around you and over you was the best possible sensation—at least when you were a fish.

Surfacing, he heard Sinbad call to the fishermen, "Farewell! And remember that this very day you met Sinbad, the greatest sailor on the seven seas!"

"Thanks for the pretty stones, mate!" the fishermen called back. "And have a nice day!"

Sinbad towed the fish toward a sandy little island, beached his boat, and pulled up the net. He slit it open and quickly worked Homer loose from the mesh. Homer clapped his fins together and opened them. A second later, he, Will, Jerome, and Maddy sat in the boat in their human form, along with several cranky-looking large fish. Sinbad flipped them into the water, and they swam away at top speed.

"It's crowded in this boat," Maddy said, looking at Sinbad. "Do you have anything to eat?"

"Sinbad!" Homer cried, putting his palms together and bowing. "I am in your debt forever, my old friend. But the day is getting late, and I must return these children to their home. How can I ever thank you?" He turned to the children. "And how can *they* thank you?" he asked. Green sparks shot from his ears.

Will got the message. "Oh, yes, thank you, Sinbad, sir!" he said, bowing over his clasped hands. "You are indeed a mighty sailor."

Jerome nodded. "Thanks a lot! Come and visit us sometime in Massachusetts!"

Even Maddy held out the ruffles of her tank suit and gave a little curtsey. "Thank you, Sinbad," she said. She turned to Will. "How bad *is* he?" she asked. "What was his sin? Did he go to jail?"

"Shhhhhh!" Will hissed. "He's a storybook character, and he's *very vain!*"

Homer was still smiling and bowing. He did this about ten more times. Giving one last "Farewell, my great and powerful friend!" he put his palms together and gently opened them from the top. The Great Barrier Reef disappeared and was replaced by the furniture in Will's room at Grandma's house.

Will looked at the alarm clock. "Omigosh! It's four a.m. here!" he whispered. "Maddy, you have to go to bed right now."

"Okay," Maddy whispered back. "I'll change out of my swimsuit first, though. Grandma might wonder where it came from."

"Hey, wait, Mad," Will said. "Thanks for saving me from the big fish. You were really brave."

"I know," Maddy said smugly. "It's the damselfish in me." She tiptoed out of the room.

"And thanks, Homer," Will said. "It was ... very ...." He searched for a word to describe the adventure. "Very surprising," he said.

Homer bowed. "My pleasure, Will. Perhaps you should send me back into the book now."

Will chanted,

"Spirit of the wind and flame,

Go now, quickly, whence you came."

He clapped his hands thrice, and Homer vanished into *The Arabian Nights*.

Will got into bed. Jerome climbed into his sleeping bag and said, "That was sooooo great."

"Jerome, you got us into a lot of trouble," Will said sternly. "Did you see the humongous fish that wanted to eat me? And what if Homer hadn't summoned Sinbad?"

"Oh, something would have saved us," Jerome said.

"Oh, yeah? Like what?" Will asked. He held Jerome's eyes till Jerome dropped his gaze.

"Okay, maybe it was dumb for me to swim away," Jerome admitted. "But we did get saved, didn't we?"

Will sighed. "Yes, we did. But, Jerome, I'm not going to let you in on any more adventures with Homer if you keep challenging him and everyone else. Sometimes it makes *sense* to follow orders."

Jerome's face fell, and Will almost felt sorry for him. There was something magnetic about Jerome's self-confidence, even when he was being a big pain.

"Well, what if I absolutely, positively know that following orders will get us into even bigger trouble? Can I challenge people then?" Jerome asked.

Will thought about it. "I guess that would be okay."

"Okay," Jerome said. "That's good enough for me."

Chapter 5

THE CHILDREN STAGGERED into the kitchen at 11:30 the next morning.

"You need brunch," Grandma said. "How late did you kids stay up?"

"I dunno, Grandma!" Jerome said cheerfully.

"Jerome, your mother called," Grandma said as she dished up bacon and eggs. "The street fair is being held today. She offered to take you kids downtown later."

Will had been to the town's street fair before with Jerome, but Maddy had never come along. "It's great,

Maddy!" Jerome said. "I'll go home after we eat and talk Mom into letting us stay there by ourselves."

Will remembered making a promise to himself the night before, when he was trapped in the fishing net. *Oh, yeah,* he thought. *I promised to find an adventure closer to home.* The street fair certainly was closer to home than the Great Barrier Reef. He decided to bring *The Arabian Nights* along, in case a chance for adventure came up at the fair.

⁓

Early in the afternoon, Will and Maddy knocked on the screen door of Jerome's house.

Aunt Nancy came to the door holding Emily. "Come in!" she said, and went off to find her car keys.

Jerome clapped his hands together and shook them over his head. "Victory! Mom is going to drop us off at the fair by ourselves." He looked at Will. "What's in the backpack?"

Aunt Nancy returned with her keys, so Will just said, "Homer." Jerome grinned, and they all piled into the van and drove off to the street fair.

"Now, I want to meet you *right* here in front of Town Hall on the dot of four," Aunt Nancy said, looking as if she meant it. Of course the children agreed.

The street fair was held on the green in the center of town. Inside the gazebo across from Town Hall, a jazz band was murdering the melody of "You Are My Sunshine."

"Are they awful or what?" Jerome asked.

"Pathetic," Will agreed. "Even their uniforms are lame." Although the day was warm, the band members wore navy suits with buttoned-up white shirts and red bowties. Their trumpets and trombones blatted tiredly along. A sign said they were THE FOUNDING FATHERS AND MOTHERS.

"They're all descended from the families who founded the town in the 1700's," Jerome explained. "They won't let anyone else join the band, and they insist on playing at every town event. Fourth of July, the Snowflake Parade—they wreck 'em all."

"But that's not fair!" Maddy said. And then she got a Look in her eye that seemed to Will to be very much like Jerome's. "Call Homer, Will! Maybe he can get the

Founding Fathers and Mothers to let some new people join the band."

Will stared at Maddy in amazement. *Is the Look a family trait?* he wondered.

"Yeah!" Jerome exclaimed. "Homer can help us teach the Founding Fathers and Mothers a lesson!"

"Okay," Will agreed. "But won't people notice him?"

"Hmmm," Jerome said. "Ask Homer to make himself unnoticeable."

A sign in the tent next to the gazebo read NEXT MAGIC SHOW 3:00. Will guessed the tent would be empty, and he was right. He ducked in and called Homer out of the book.

"Good afternoon, Will," Homer said with his usual bow. "May I grant your heart's truest wish?"

Will shook his head. "Not yet, Homer. This wish isn't really for me—it's for Jerome's town." He told Homer all about the Founding Fathers and Mothers. "Can you think of a way to get them to change their minds about letting new people join the band? Oh, and you also have to make yourself unnoticeable somehow."

Homer beamed. "Of course I can do those things! First I will make myself less visible. That is one of the oldest tricks in the book, as they say. You've read about it in *Alice's Adventures in Wonderland*, no doubt."

Homer put his hands together and lifted them upward. Suddenly he was holding a small bottle labeled DRINK ME.

Will remembered that in *Alice in Wonderland*, Alice checked her DRINK ME bottle to make sure it wasn't poison before she drank the contents. Homer did the same, sniffing the liquid carefully. Then he put the bottle to his mouth and chugged the potion down. *Poof!* He vanished in a swirling haze of green smoke.

Will looked around.

"Down here!" Homer called in a teeny little voice. Will looked down. The top of Homer's bald, green head was sticking out of Will's shirt pocket. Homer had shrunk himself down to three inches. He was the size of one of Will's fingers.

Will found Jerome and Maddy near the bandstand. "Notice anything different about me?" he asked.

Jerome and Maddy studied him. "Omigosh!" Jerome exclaimed, pointing. "You shrank Homer!"

"He shrank himself," Will said. "He used a bottle labeled DRINK ME."

"Ooh, like the one in *Alice in Wonderland*?" Maddy said, and Will remembered that it was his sister's favorite book.

"Yeah. Okay, what happens next?" Will asked.

The Founding Fathers and Mothers were taking a break. "I think *we* can play better than them," Maddy said. "Should we try?"

"We'll be a jazz trio!" Will said. "Me on clarinet, you on keyboard, and Jerome on—what instrument do you play, Jerome? I forget."

"Trumpet, but you never heard me play," Jerome pointed out. "Homer had better make us *much* better musicians than we are right now."

"Please turn us into a *really* good jazz trio, Homer," Will requested.

"Certainly. Let me see . . . jazz musicians. I once had one for a master, and I whiled away some idle moments reading his album covers." Homer stuck his tiny hands out of Will's pocket and touched them together.

Will, Jerome, and Maddy appeared on the gazebo bandstand. They were dressed all in black—black T-shirts and jeans, black sunglasses. A sign declared that they were the WONDERLAND TRIO.

Will held a clarinet with glistening silver keys. Maddy was seated at the keyboard, and Jerome had a gleaming trumpet in his hands. Will looked at his clarinet in amazement. There were so many songs crowding his brain that he hardly knew where to begin. His fingers itched to play them all.

He looked down at Homer. "What'd you do?"

"I have given you the knowledge of Benny Goodman, one of the best clarinetists who ever lived," Homer explained. "Jerome has the talents of the famous trumpet player, Louis Armstrong, while Maddy has the gifts of the pianist and band leader, Duke Ellington."

"Wow, thanks!" Will said.

As band leader, Maddy took charge. "Okay, trio, we'll start with 'Take the A Train,'" she announced. "A-one, a-two, a-one-two-three-four!"

Will couldn't believe how good they sounded. Neither could the people standing nearby. A crowd began forming around the gazebo.

"Hey! You kids get down from there!" yelled one of the Founding Mothers.

"Let the Wonderland Trio play!" someone called. "They're terrific!"

The Founding Mother jumped on the stage, waving her saxophone in the air. "I insist that you gatecrashers stop playing right now!" she said. "You aren't even on the program! No other band can be!"

"Boooooo!" the crowd shouted at the Founding Mother. "Get down!" The trio went right on playing.

"Aw, go soak your saxophone reed," added a young man in the crowd.

"Do you know who I am, young man?" the Founding Mother asked, shaking her sax at him.

"Yeah! You Founding Fusspots have had a monopoly on music in this town for too long!" the man said. "It's time for some new blood!" The crowd cheered.

"Really!" fumed the Founding Mother, getting very red in the face.

"Trumpet solo, Doctor J!" Maddy said. Jerome stood up and began playing a flawless solo.

"Wow!" said the crowd, swaying in time to Jerome's music.

"Could that be *Nancy Lewis's* son?" someone asked, pointing at Jerome. "He's certainly improved since the fifth-grade band concert!"

Even the Founding Mother was silenced. After a moment, she got off the stage and joined the crowd. When the song ended, she clapped along with everyone else.

"Perhaps we *could* use some new talent in our band," she was heard to say. "Do you think that very short trumpet player is available?"

The jazz trio played a few more tunes and finished up with a version of "When the Saints Go Marching In" that had the crowd clapping their hands and stamping their feet.

"Thank you. Thank you," Maddy murmured as the trio bowed. "And now, if you'll excuse us, we need to take a break."

They had to run away from the crowd in the end. "Whew!" Jerome panted, sinking behind a tree. "It's hard work being popular!"

When they sat down, Will found he couldn't think about anything except the clarinet he was still holding. He couldn't wait to get back onstage. Maddy was playing the piano in the air, and Jerome was fingering his trumpet absentmindedly.

"Homer, I think we'd better lose our talents before our next adventure," he said. The others nodded sadly.

With a lift of his hands, Homer made the instruments vanish and changed the trio back into their regular clothes, and Will found he could think about ordinary things again.

"I'm thirsty," Maddy announced. They went looking for something cold to drink.

A vendor was selling lemonade, and the children stopped to buy three frosty glasses. Will drained his drink and pointed to the sign for a show that was assembling nearby. "Let's watch Barney Lutz and His Trained Mutts."

Barney Lutz's four little dogs jumped through hoops, skipped rope, balanced balls on their noses, and even walked a tightrope. The crowd yelled and clapped. At the end of the show, a tall woman with wisps of white hair escaping from her bun went up to Barney Lutz. She was holding a fluffy white cat.

Jerome pointed to the cat's owner. "That's Mrs. Heffernan," he explained. "Grandma knows her. She's in charge of the street fair this year. And, um"— he lowered his voice and tapped his head—"she's a little eccentric, you know, wacky. She goes everywhere with her cat, Snugglepuss."

Mrs. Heffernan set the cat down so she could shake Barney Lutz's hand. "You're a hit, Barney!" she said. "How can we thank you?"

Barney Lutz's dogs were far too well trained to snap at Snugglepuss, Will noticed. They sat quietly and let the cat hiss at them.

"Um, Mrs. Heffernan?" Jerome said. "I don't think your cat likes Barney's dogs."

Mrs. Heffernan turned to smile at him. "Oh, hello, Jerome, dear. Please tell your grandmother that we missed her today at the Garden Club sale. Now, are these the cousins I've heard so much about?"

"Oh, yeah, this is Will and that's Maddy. They're visiting for two weeks. But Mrs. Heffernan, look at your cat—"

"How do you do?" Will said politely to Mrs. Heffernan.

She reached for his hand, beaming. "What a pleasure to meet you, Will! And little Maddy, too! Please feel free to pet Snugglepuss."

Snugglepuss was openly taunting the dogs now, parading up and down in front of them and growling. Bending down, Will held his fingers about a foot from the cat. "Nice kitty?" he said. Snugglepuss lunged at his hand, and he snatched it away again.

Will heard a soft thud and realized that Homer had fallen out of his pocket. The cat pounced. The next thing Will knew, Snugglepuss was running away. And Homer was dangling by one arm from the cat's mouth!

"Oh, my darling puddums girl has run away!" Mrs. Heffernan said. "And I have *so* much to do directing the street fair!"

"We'll get him, I mean her, back to you somehow, Mrs. Heffernan!" Will promised. He grabbed Jerome and Maddy by the hand and dragged them a few feet away, where nobody could overhear them.

He pointed. "The cat has Homer!" he whispered.

"Oh, no!" Jerome and Maddy gasped. All three children raced after the cat.

"Why doesn't Homer use his magic to escape?" Maddy asked as they ran.

"The cat is holding Homer by one arm," Will said. "I bet he can't get his hands together to work his magic."

Snugglepuss crossed the street and disappeared into a shaded alleyway between two buildings. At the end of the alley, the cat sat down and bent her head to lower

Homer till he was within reach of her paws. Lazily, the cat began batting Homer from one side to the other.

Will inched toward the cat. Snugglepuss switched her tail angrily against the alley pavement. Then, with Homer still in her mouth, she leapt toward a fire escape and ran swiftly to the top.

Will looked up. The flights of narrow, rusty stairs led to a small platform outside a third-story window. The cat was sitting on the platform—*and dangling Homer over the edge!*

"I'm coming, Homer!" Will said. He began climbing the rusted stairs, holding tightly to the top rung of the railing and trying to ignore the gap between the lower rung and the steps. The space was definitely big enough for someone Will's size to fall through.

Jerome started up after him, but Will motioned him back. "You and Maddy stay down in case you need to catch Homer!" he said.

"Here, kitty, kitty," he called when he reached the top of the first flight of stairs. The cat swiped a paw at Homer.

Will gulped and started up the second flight, forcing himself not to look down. At the top of the flight, he rested. Then, with shuddering breaths, he climbed the last flight of steps. A few steps below the platform, his foot slipped. Losing his grasp on the railing, he fell heavily to his knees. His head pitched sideways, and he glimpsed the faraway pavement through the enormous gap.

Will's throat filled with a sour, throw-up taste, and he swallowed it down. Clinging to the railing's bottom rung, he tried to climb a step on one knee, but something was stopping him. His shoelace had caught on the railing's ironwork. He would have to let go of the railing to free himself.

Will closed his eyes, feeling dizzy, and rested his head against a step.

"Psst! Will!"

He opened his eyes. There was Jerome, untying Will's shoelace from a few steps below. "Wow, am I glad to see you," Will whispered.

Jerome grinned and retied Will's newly freed sneaker. "Good thing I didn't follow orders, huh? Good luck. I'd better get out of here before we spook the cat." He started creeping back down the fire escape.

Will pulled himself up to the platform. The cat arched her back and growled without letting go of Homer. Her fur puffed up till she looked twice her size.

"Nice kitty," Will said. "Homer, are you okay? Can you *talk* to the cat?"

"I am well, thank you," replied Homer faintly. "And I have tried talking to Snugglepuss. She tells me she does not, as a rule, converse with her meals. A sound piece of etiquette, by the way, made famous in Lewis Carroll's *Through the Looking Glass.*"

"Yeah. Here's my plan," Will said. "I'll try to grab the cat. I just want to make her drop you. You'll probably fall. Can you work your magic before you hit the ground?"

"If my hands are freed, I shall do my best," Homer said.

Will looked down into the shaded gloom of the alley. Maddy and Jerome were standing below, looking up anxiously and holding out their hands.

Will inched forward on his elbows and knees. He grabbed at Snugglepuss and touched fur, but the cat slipped from his grasp and raced back down the steps.

Will peered over the edge of the fire escape, afraid of what he'd see.

Homer was floating gently toward the ground beneath the fabric of a miniature green parachute. As Will watched, the parachute drifted into Maddy's outstretched hands.

"All right!" he yelled. His shaky knees gave way, and he collapsed on the platform. How was *he* going to get down again?

"Uh, Homer . . . ?" he said faintly, not expecting the genie to hear him.

"Homer says to hold on tight!" Jerome called. Will did. The fire escape curled up around him, forming a steep, three-story slide. Will began slipping down it, wondering as he picked up speed how he'd stop himself at the bottom. Peeking over his sneakers, he saw a giant green pillow ahead. He hit the pillow with an explosion of green feathers.

"Hooray!" Jerome and Maddy cheered, thumping Will on the back. Maddy carefully put Homer back in her brother's pocket.

Will checked his watch. "Oh, no! It's five to four! Homer, we have to be back in front of Town Hall in exactly five minutes. I left my backpack with *The Arabian Nights* in it by the lemonade stand, and we have to return Snugglepuss to Mrs. Heffernan!"

Homer nodded. "Quite all right." With a lifting motion of his hands, Homer summoned the backpack. It came zipping through the air and landed at Will's feet.

Maddy whispered, "Wow! Do you think he reads the same books as Harry Potter?"

"Now, the cat." Homer looked thoughtful for a moment. Then he touched his hands together and lifted them heavenward. "Snugglepuss is back with Mrs. Heffernan," he said. "She is far fonder of her pet than the cat deserves, as can be said of so many of us who walk upon this Earth."

At exactly one minute before four, Homer transported the children to Town Hall. Homer was so small that Will figured nobody would notice if he sent him back to *The Arabian Nights* in broad daylight. Homer whooshed out of Will's pocket and into the book just as Aunt Nancy's van pulled up.

"Jerome, I got the strangest call from your friend Kevin's mom," Aunt Nancy said as they drove away.

"She wants to know the name of your trumpet teacher. Now, why would she ask that?"

"I dunno, Mom!" Jerome replied. "I think she mixed me up with this guy from the Wonderland Trio."

"Take it away, Doctor J!" Maddy said innocently, and they all started to laugh.

Chapter 6

THE NEXT MORNING, Will came into the kitchen to find Grandma sitting by the phone and staring off into space. "Good morning, dear! Meant to make you pecan waffles, but I got so distracted when Maxine called—" Grandma abruptly stopped talking.

"Why did you get distracted when Mom called?" Will asked. He poured himself some orange juice.

"Might as well tell you. Your mother didn't say I couldn't, and I'd be glad for the chance to talk it over," Grandma said. "Here's what happened, Will:

your parents paid an artist friend to hand-letter a beautiful sign that said, MAXINE'S: OPEN DURING CONSTRUCTION. COME AND TASTE OUR HOMEMADE BAKED GOODS! They put it out for the first time yesterday, and by closing time, it had disappeared."

"Did the people at Coffee Island *steal* the sign?" Will asked.

"That's what your parents think," Grandma said. "Can't prove it, but it's the only explanation they can think of. They told the police, but the tall, friendly policeman who usually patrols the mall is on vacation. His substitute didn't seem to think there was anything worth investigating."

Maddy walked into the kitchen, yawning. She had heard Grandma's last words. "We know someone who could substitute for the policeman," she said, grinning at Will.

"Well, until he returns, I don't think Maxine and your dad are going to get their sign back," Grandma said. "They tried calling the chief of police, but he didn't call back. I'm sure he thinks it's just a kid's prank. Unfortunately, your parents think otherwise."

After breakfast, Grandma settled into a comfortable

chair and put her leg up on a footstool. "Got to a really exciting point in my mystery," she said. "You kids don't need me right now, do you?"

After assuring Grandma that they were fine, Will called Jerome. "Emergency," he whispered, cupping the mouthpiece of the phone. "Can you be here in ten minutes?"

"*Ten?* One!" Jerome exclaimed and hung up. One minute later, he was standing on the doorstep with his skateboard under his arm.

The three children huddled in Will's room. "Here's the thing," Will said. "I really think we should use Homer's magic to go to Commerce today. Mom and Dad need us." He explained about the missing sign. "It sounds to me like Coffee Island is behind this. We need to find out for sure."

"So how would Homer help?" Jerome wanted to know. "I mean, you could just tell him to find out who stole the sign. Why should we go to your town?"

"Because we don't just want to know what's going on. We need to find out *why* it's going on, and then stop it for good," Will explained. "I was thinking we could dress Homer up like that policeman he looks like, and then we'd all do some snooping around. What do you guys think?"

"Homer could distract the people at Coffee Island," Jerome suggested. "And then we could sneak behind the counter and look for the sign."

"That's pretty much what I was thinking," said Will. "We'll just have to disguise Homer really, really well."

Maddy asked, "Won't Grandma notice if we all disappear for a while?"

"Good point," Will said. "She's buried pretty deep in her mystery. What if we tell her we want to go fly kites on the beach? I think she'd trust us down there by ourselves at low tide, as long as we say we won't go near the water." He told himself that tomorrow, he *really* would fly a kite to make the lie come true. But this was important. They had to save Maxine's!

$\sim\!\!e\!\!\sim\!\!9\!\!\sim$

Grandma sent them to the backyard shed to find kites. "Have fun, kids!" she called, smiling at them before sneaking a longing look at her mystery.

Back in his room, Will reached under his pillow for *The Arabian Nights* and flipped to the story of the fisherman and the genie. He put his hand on the picture of Homer. "I need a genius!" he said. Homer whooshed out of the picture.

"Greetings, Will, Jerome, Maddy." Homer, ever polite, put his hands together and bowed. "You have not yet achieved your heart's truest wish, Will, or you would not be calling me today."

Will felt a little uncomfortable. Was Homer hinting that it was about time he set the genie free?

No, Will decided, *Homer's just stating the facts. You're the one who doesn't know what your heart's truest wish is.*

"Homer, we have a big problem, and I think you can help," Will said. He explained to Homer all about Maxine's Diner and the competition from Coffee Island. He told Homer about the fifty-cent price cut on coffee-and-a-danish at Coffee Island, and now the disappearance of the sign.

"So we'd like to make a quick trip to my hometown, Commerce, New York," Will explained. "You'll need to disguise yourself. You look a lot like the mall policeman, but you need to dress like him and maybe shrink a bit."

"Ah!" Homer said. "I do know how to look like a policeman, of the 1970's, at least. My last master had a difficult request: to find a parking spot in New York City. I was glad to oblige, by dressing up as a most persuasive policeman."

"There you go!" Jerome said. "What are we waiting for?"

Homer bowed to Will. "I await your wish, Will."

Will looked around at his sister and cousin. "Let's put our kites down before we go," he suggested, and they did.

"I want all of us—Maddy, Jerome, Homer, and me— to be at the mall in Commerce. Homer should look like the mall policeman. And somehow my parents shouldn't notice we're there."

Homer closed his hands and opened them from the top. Instantly the four of them were standing in the Commerce mall. And Homer really had become a policeman! He wore mirrored sunglasses and a cap with a visor, and his uniform had a badge that read COMMERCE POLICE DEPARTMENT. He had shrunk his height, too, Will decided. Homer wasn't an inch taller than seven feet now. He was still greenish, but somehow, it wasn't the first thing you noticed about him.

Will, Maddy, and Jerome were all wearing baseball caps pulled low over their faces. Will took off his cap and studied it. He seemed to be rooting for the New York Yankees, Maddy was for the Chicago Cubs, and Jerome was for the Atlanta Braves. Homer had no doubt conjured up the caps to help them pass Maxine's unnoticed, but he'd picked three teams that were fierce rivals of Will's team, the Mets. *What on Earth has Homer been reading?* Will wondered, then shrugged and jammed the cap back on his head.

Will peered longingly inside the window of Maxine's. His mother was washing a coffee pot, and his father was wiping down the counter. It was all Will could do not to walk inside and tell them everything.

Maddy obviously felt the same way. "Mommy!" she yelled. Will and Jerome each grabbed one of her hands and began walking her across the mall toward Coffee Island. But when Will glanced back, he saw that their mother was coming toward the window of the diner, looking puzzled.

"Quick, Homer!" he said.

"I am on top of the situation, Will." Homer closed and opened his hands. A small storm cloud appeared over the diner and poured forth blinding sheets of rain.

"How'd you do that?" Will asked as he watched his mother turn away from the window. The rain dried up and the cloud disappeared.

"I was a great fan of the old comic strip *Li'l Abner*," Homer explained. "One of the characters, Joe Btfsplk, had a permanent rain cloud over his head. I just summoned Joe's cloud."

They faced Coffee Island. Jerome pointed to a sign in the store window. "Whoa, decaf-choca-java shakes! Can I get one?"

"That sounds yummy," Will said. "I didn't bring any money, though. Darn!"

"You only have to wish for money, and you will be well provided for," Homer told him.

Will nodded and took a deep breath. "Okay, let's go," he said. He held the door open to let Maddy, Jerome, and Homer inside.

Will hung back near the door and looked around. He saw round tables and chairs, tasteful displays of coffees and teas from around the world, and a large, curving metal counter. Behind it stood two people in white aprons and caps that said COFFEE ISLAND—THE START OF A GREAT TASTE ADVENTURE. Will guessed that the fancy metal machines that bubbled and hissed were coffee makers, espresso makers, and decaf-choca-java shake makers.

The walls were decorated with a mural of sand dunes lapped by thundering waves. Here and there pine trees dotted the shore, and on one wall, a skeleton with a gleaming gold tooth held up a Coffee Island mug. Half-buried in the sand next to the skeleton was a treasure chest filled with bags of Coffee Island coffee beans. Behind him, a sailing ship sported a pirate flag—the Jolly Roger.

Homer looked around and nodded admiringly. "I've been inside many books," he said, "and Will, looking at this place, it's almost as if I'd stepped inside *Treasure Island,* with some added coffee flavoring."

"They're supposed to be the *enemy,*" Will whispered. "You're not supposed to like them!"

One of the coffee servers looked like a college student. Auburn hair spilled out from under her cap in an untidy bun. The other salesperson, a tall, gangly man who wore a red shirt and lime green pants beneath his apron, was clearly her manager. He was chewing out the college student, whose name (according to a tag she wore) was NICOLE.

"I've told you over and over," the manager was whining, "we don't have *time* to clean the pots with every brewing. Just sell coffee. That's what they're paying us for."

Nicole seemed to be rather spunky. She stood up tall and said, "Well, *I* took Coffee Island's orientation class, Jim—I mean, Mr. Vito—and we're supposed to wash the pot before every brewing. It's right in the employee booklet, written by our Cee-Ee-Oh."

Just as Will was wondering what a Cee-Ee-Oh was, Maddy tugged on Homer's elbow and asked him the same question. "That would be the chief executive officer, I believe, Maddy," Homer said. "The person who runs the organization."

Will hoped Nicole would win the argument. At Maxine's, the coffee pots were always carefully washed between brewings.

But Mr. Vito leaned toward Nicole and rolled his

eyes. "Jeepers, Nicole. I, for one, don't plan to work at Coffee Island for the rest of my life. Who cares what the employee booklet says?"

Nicole frowned. "Well, Coffee Island has certain standards, and *I* think we should uphold them." Just then, she noticed the customers standing by the door.

Mr. Vito saw them, too. "Ugh, kids! They never know what they want to order. You wait on them, and I'll handle the officer."

"Hi!" Nicole called cheerfully. "Can I help you kids?"

Will hesitated, realizing that he hadn't thought about exactly *how* they would find his parents' sign. He was pretty sure that if any dirty doings had gone on, they were Mr. Vito's. He didn't believe Nicole could possibly be a villain. She reminded him too much of his mother.

He walked forward. "Hi," he said. "Yes, we'd like three decaf-choca-java shakes, please."

"What would *you* like, Officer?" Mr. Vito asked in a fakely nice voice.

"I believe I'd like a word with you," Homer said pleasantly.

As Nicole turned her back to make the frozen shakes, Will edged around the side of the counter to draw her into conversation. He flapped his hands toward Jerome and Maddy, signaling them to go around the other end of the counter. It led to a door with a sign that read, EMPLOYEES ONLY. Jerome arched an eyebrow at Will, then grabbed Maddy's hand and began tiptoeing toward the back room.

"Uh—Nicole!" Will said. He wasn't used to talking to people twice his age.

"Mm-hmh?" Nicole asked. She looked to make sure that Mr. Vito wasn't watching, then slid the nearly empty decaf coffee pot off its burner and thrust it under a faucet. Will watched as she scrubbed it out, rinsed it, and put it back on the burner.

"Um . . . " Will tried to think up some coffee chat. "What's your favorite kind of coffee?"

"Oh, you're interested in coffee?" Nicole flipped a switch to start brewing a new pot of decaf coffee.

"Well, not the caffeinated kind," Will said. "My parents don't let me drink that. But I kind of like decaf coffee shakes." He hoped Nicole couldn't tell that this would be the first one he'd ever tasted.

Nicole nodded. "We have some terrific decafs. I like our breakfast brews, personally. The other kinds— French roasts and all—they're too strong for me. Unless I have exams, and then I chug them nonstop. *With* caffeine."

"What are you studying?" Will asked. The decaf coffee pot was full. He watched as Nicole poured the coffee over shaved ice into three tall cups, then added chocolate syrup and milk. One at a time, she put the cups under a blender.

"Psychology," Nicole said. "What makes people tick."

Will nodded absent-mindedly. He'd noticed that Homer and Mr. Vito were talking in front of the counter. "But, Mr. Vito," he heard Homer say, "why should I not be allowed to look for the sign? If the sign is not here, why should you mind if I search the premises?"

"I'm innocent until proven guilty, that's why!" Mr. Vito said. "Show me a search warrant, or get off this property!"

At that moment, Jerome and Maddy emerged from the back room—carrying a large, hand-lettered sign.

They lugged it to the middle of the coffee shop and set it down with a thump.

"Homer, look!" Will yelled. Everyone turned to look at Will. He pointed to the sign.

"Ha! We caught you red-handed," Jerome said.

Will was sure from Mr. Vito's stricken expression that *he* was the one who had stolen the sign and hidden it in the back room.

But all Mr. Vito said was, "Where did you find that sign, children? I never saw it before in my life." He pretended to yawn and studied his fingernails.

Will was so angry he could hardly talk. "You—you—liar!" he sputtered. "You stole the sign from Maxine's! You *are* a dirty, low-down coffee crook!"

Mr. Vito glanced at his watch. "Are you all through now?" he said. "Oh, yes, your shakes, of course. Have you paid for them, children? No? They're on me. Why don't you enjoy them outside? Officer—" He looked at Homer. "Did you tell me your name?"

"Officer Homer," Homer replied.

"Officer Homer," said Mr. Vito, "I believe this is the sign you were looking for. I have no idea how it got into our back room, but I suspect Nicole put it there."

Nicole was holding the last shake. She slapped it down on the counter so hard, half of it spilled out. "Now, look here, Jim Vito, I've put up with a lot from you. But I'm not going to stand here and listen to you insult my integrity! No job is worth that. I QUIT!" She tore off her cap and apron and threw them on the counter.

"Fine," Mr. Vito said. "Now I won't have to fire you."

Nicole's mouth twitched downward. Will could see that she was trying not to cry. He tried to think of a way to regain control of the situation. There must be *something* they could do to help Nicole—and Maxine's, too.

Maddy crept around the counter and took Nicole's hand. "Don't cry! Maybe we can help you." She pointed to Homer. "He's magic."

Nicole smiled sadly. "I don't think so. Not unless he can call up the CEO of Coffee Island for me. Nobody else could save me right now."

"That's it!" Will said. "Great idea, Nicole!"

Mr. Vito scowled at them. "What *are* you talking about?" he asked crossly. Will ignored him.

"Homer, please summon the CEO of Coffee Island,"

Will said. "I don't know his name—does that matter?"

"His name is Jacob Wexler," Nicole said. She looked from Will to Homer hopefully. "What, are you going to conference-call him?"

"I will do better than that," Homer promised. "I will give you Mr. Wexler himself." He touched his hands together and raised them toward heaven.

Chapter 7

A BALDING MAN with a little mustache and a double-breasted suit came in the door.

"Was I doing a spot inspection today?" he asked himself. "I thought I was attending a sales conference for the southwest region. Oh, dear! My wife is right. I really need to cut back on my business travel."

He looked around the shop and spotted Mr. Vito. "Hello, there!" he said. "I'm Jake Wexler, your CEO. You're the manager, I see!

How are things here in—" he paused. "Where *am* I?"

"Commerce, New York," said Mr. Vito. "Things are fine, Mr. Wexler. Just fine! We're so glad you could visit us today!"

Nicole quickly put her apron and cap back on. She put out her hand for Mr. Wexler to shake. "My name is Nicole Stavinski, Mr. Wexler, and I'm very pleased to meet you. In fact, you are my personal hero, if you don't mind my saying so."

"Enchanted," murmured Mr. Wexler. He looked a little happier at having been transported across the country and plunked down unexpectedly in one of his stores.

"But, Mr. Wexler, I'm sorry to say that things aren't fine here in Commerce," Nicole said bravely. "In fact, they're pretty awful."

"Don't listen to this girl!" Mr. Vito said, stepping in front of Nicole. "She's a psychology student, and she's delusional!"

Jerome poked Will. "Get Homer onto Mr. Vito, fast!" he whispered.

Will sidled over to Homer. "Homer, please find a way to distract Mr. Vito so that Nicole can talk to

Mr. Wexler," he asked. Homer thought for a second, then closed his palms and opened them with a lifting motion. Will wondered why Homer needed magic to keep Mr. Vito away from Nicole.

Taking the manager by the arm, Homer said something that sounded strangely familiar to Will. "Now, you look here: you're young, you are, but you're as smart as paint."

Mr. Vito smiled for the first time. "Why, thank you, Officer Homer."

"I've taken a notion into my own numskull," Homer said, smiling delightedly at Mr. Vito. "Let's have a cup of coffee and talk it over." He caught Nicole's eye and winked.

Nicole poured Homer and Mr. Vito each a cup of Today's Special Brew. "Milk and sugar are over there," she said, pointing.

"Very good, you're putting the customer first, Nicole!" said Mr. Wexler. "Now, what's all this about things not being right?"

Putting her elbows on the shiny metal counter, Nicole took a deep breath and began to talk. Will had to admire her. Maybe it was because she was studying psychology, but she had a neat way of laying out the facts.

"Ah—" Mr. Vito said, sounding rather alarmed. "I think I should talk to Mr. Wexler before that young lady says too much to him."

"We'll just be a few minutes," Homer assured him. As they walked to the station with the milk and sugar, Homer continued holding on to Mr. Vito's arm. But he developed a rolling gait, as if he were leaning heavily on a crutch. Will stared. Was that a parrot on Homer's shoulder?

"Pieces of eight! Pieces of eight!" the parrot said.

After helping himself to milk and sugar, Homer undulated over to one of the round tables and sat down with Mr. Vito. Will couldn't hear everything they were saying, but Homer seemed to be giving Mr. Vito a good talking to. "Duty is duty, mate!" he thundered, while the parrot singsonged, "It's duty, mate! Pieces of eight!"

Will looked at Jerome and mouthed, "What's going on?"

Jerome took Maddy's hand and led her over to Will. "Here's what I think," he whispered, drawing

Will and Maddy to him in a huddle. "Did you ever read *Treasure Island?*"

"Of course! That's where the weird things Homer is saying are coming from!" Will said. "He's talking like Long John Silver. But why is he pretending to be a pirate?"

"This is my theory," Jerome said. "Homer is a nice guy. He doesn't really know how to act like a villain, so he's borrowing one from a book. You know, he's—"

"He's a book genie," Will and Maddy chimed in.

"If you like the service, well, you'll join," Homer was telling Mr. Vito. "And if you don't, Jim, why, you're free to answer no—free and welcome, shipmate; and if fairer can be said by mortal seaman, shiver my sides!"

"Shiver my sides. Awwwk!" the parrot squawked.

"Do you think we'll get to keep the parrot when this is over?" Maddy asked.

The other grown-ups hadn't noticed Homer's strange transformation from a policeman into a pirate. "Mr. Wexler," Nicole was saying, "at our training we learned to put our customers first, to brew a good cup of coffee, and to be good neighbors. But I'm afraid Mr. Vito doesn't do *any* of those things. In fact, he's very bad at them."

She described how Mr. Vito didn't like waiting on young people and how he never washed out the coffee pot between brewings. "Sometimes he grinds the coffee all at once at the beginning of the week, to save time," she added.

Mr. Wexler sank into a chair. "These are serious charges," he said. "Nicole, please pour me an extravaganté-size cup of today's special brew. I'll have to investigate this myself."

Nicole nodded, turned around, and expertly poured Mr. Wexler's coffee. Mr. Wexler took a sip and grimaced. "Made from stale grounds!" he announced.

"But there's something much, much worse going on here," Nicole said. She told Mr. Wexler about the coffee war with Maxine's. "First he lowered the prices to beat the coffee shop's," she said. "Then he stole their sign—that sign sitting right over there. Mr. Wexler, I'm sorry to say that Mr. Vito hasn't been a good neighbor here in Commerce."

Mr. Wexler stroked the ends of his mustache.

"Mr. Vito, do you have anything to say for yourself?" he asked.

Just as the grown-ups turned their attention in the direction of Mr. Vito and Homer, the parrot disappeared from Homer's shoulder and he relaxed his grip on Mr. Vito's forearm.

"What's that?" Mr. Vito asked, rubbing his arm.

"I said, *Do you have anything to say for yourself?*" Mr. Wexler stood up and crossed his arms.

"Oh. Uh, no, Mr. Wexler. I don't have anything to say," Mr. Vito said.

"Mr. Vito, I'm sorry to say that you're fired," Mr. Wexler told him. "I'll give you two weeks' pay to help you find another job. I suggest you avoid the food service industry. You really aren't cut out for it."

"No," Mr. Vito said dreamily. "No. In fact, I always wanted to be a merchant sailor. That's why I came to work at Coffee Island. At least it *reminds* me of the sea. This officer here"—he pointed to Homer—"reawakened that dream." He sighed. "But I can't go to sea. It's hopeless."

"Why not?" Nicole asked.

"Promise not to laugh," Mr. Vito said. "Here it is:

I can't pass the color test. I can't tell red from green."

"*That's* why he dresses that way!" Maddy blurted.

"I'm color-blind myself," said Mr. Wexler in a sympathetic voice. "I couldn't tell the difference between my red and green crayons at school. Other children made fun of me. That's when I got the idea to start a business and be my own boss."

Will sidled over to Homer. "I can't stand it, Homer. Could you just give Mr. Vito the ability to tell colors apart, please?"

"Indeed, Will! Let's stow this talk," Homer said, putting his hands together and lifting them up.

Mr. Vito looked around the room in a puzzled way. "Why, Nicole—you're a redhead!" he exclaimed. Then he looked down at his clothes. "These colors clash terribly, don't they?"

"Jim, you can tell red from green!" Nicole said. "I mean, I don't have *green* hair."

A look of pure happiness covered Mr. Vito's face. He turned to Homer and pumped his hand up and down. "You've done me a good turn, Officer, you and your—wasn't there a parrot here a minute ago? Well, anyway—thanks."

Homer smiled. "You couldn't say more, I'm sure, sir, not if you was my mother," he said.

"He's still being Long John Silver from *Treasure Island*," Jerome muttered. "I wish I could bring Homer to school for my book talks."

Mr. Vito gave Nicole a hug and then shook Mr. Wexler's hand. "Good-bye, everyone! I'm off to the bounding main!" He put his apron and cap on the counter and sprinted out the door.

Mr. Wexler turned to Nicole. "I'm promoting you to manager of the store, Nicole. Please start by grinding some fresh coffee beans and brewing some fresh pots." He pulled out a handkerchief and wiped his forehead. "What a day! I could really use a cup of coffee right this minute. I can't wait until Nicole gets those new pots brewed. Say, Officer, do you know where I can get some good coffee in this town?"

"I certainly do, Mr. Wexler," Homer said, pointing. "Right across the street, at Maxine's. Why don't you return their sign, while you're at it?"

"Excellent idea!" Mr. Wexler said.

Will heard the rest of the story from his parents when they called Grandma's house that night.

"You'll never believe who walked into our store today!" Mom exclaimed.

"Try me," Will said.

His mother said that Mr. Wexler had been very nice about the sign. "He apologized and said that Mr. Vito would no longer be a problem. Then he asked for a cup of coffee. Guess what happened next! I'll let your father tell you."

Will's dad got on the phone. "Hey, Will!" he said. "Listen to this. Mr. Wexler took one sip of your mom's coffee, and he swooned. He said he'd never tasted anything so good—not even in any of his own stores! And he said that he'd started to wonder if he was losing his mind that day, till he sipped Maxine's coffee and he knew that everything was going to be just fine. He drank the first cup down and asked for another. After he'd drained that, he said he was hiring your mom as a consultant. She'll travel to his regional sales conferences—just four trips a year—to advise the top salespeople on brewing a great cup of coffee, putting the customer first, and—oh, I forget the last thing now—"

"Being a good neighbor?" Will suggested.

"That's it," Dad said. "But here's the best thing of all, Will. He's paying your mother so much that we've hired our old staff back, with raises for both of them. We're coming to Grandma's house for a vacation after all!"

Late that night, after the plans had been made for Mom and Dad to come up to Grandma's house on Saturday and stay a week, Will put on his pajamas and brushed his teeth. Then he went to his room and closed the door. He took *The Arabian Nights* out from under his pillow and put his hand on the picture of the genie. "I need a genius!" he said softly.

Whoosh! Homer appeared before him. Will threw his arms around the genie's large green waist. "We did it, Homer!" he said. He explained all the good things that had happened after they had left Coffee Island.

"That is very, very good, Will," Homer said. "Have I granted your heart's truest wish?"

Will shut his eyes and scrunched up his face.

No answer came to him. He opened his eyes again. "I don't know. So much has happened, but nothing stands out."

"Is there anything you still require?" Homer prompted him.

"The blue bug!" Will remembered. "It belongs by the highway in Providence, and it isn't there."

"Ah," Homer said, "I believe a newspaper is what you need." He closed and opened his hands. He was holding a newspaper with a headline that read BUG TAKES A TRIP TO THE ZOO. Will studied the picture of the bug, surrounded by adoring children. He read how the bug was just visiting the zoo for a while. It would be back in place by the end of the summer.

Homer watched him carefully. As always, the genie's face did not show impatience, but a little puff of green smoke crept from the top of his head and formed a heart, then faded away.

I'm being selfish, Will thought. *I should just say I got my heart's truest wish, and let Homer go looking for his wife.* Locating the bug hadn't really been his heart's truest wish, though.

He thought about all the things that had happened

since he had met Homer. Maddy and Jerome had both turned into surprisingly good company—not just good, but great. He'd been flying and boogie boarding, and he'd even gotten to visit the Great Barrier Reef. Maxine's Diner was safe, and his parents were coming up to Grandma's for their vacation, after all.

"I guess there never was just *one* wish," Will said. "I wanted this trip to Grandma's to turn out okay, in lots of different ways, and it did. It's been better than okay. It's been fantastic, Homer. Thank you." A thought struck him. "Does that count as my heart's truest wish?" he asked. "You can still be free, and go looking for your wife, right?"

"We will test this," Homer said. "You can only command me until I've granted your heart's truest wish. If I have already answered your wish, you will have no more power over me. Make a wish, Will."

"I wish I had my own cell phone," Will said off the top of his head. He waited as Homer cupped his palms and opened them. No cell phone appeared.

"That's okay. I can go on borrowing Dad's phone," Will said. "I just play games on it, anyway."

Homer put out his hand and gave Will a hearty

handshake. Then he clapped Will on the shoulders. "I shouldn't have favorites, Will, but you were the best friend of all the hundred masters I served. And now I must be off."

"Wait a minute!" Will said. He didn't want Homer to go. "Um, how will you know where to find your wife?"

"I know exactly where she is," Homer said. "She's safe in the same brass jewelry box that she's been trapped in for three thousand years. The box lies within a tel, an ancient hill in Israel. I have only to wish myself there, and to wish her free."

Will pictured Homer freeing his wife after three thousand years, and he had to smile, even though he felt sad. "Okay, Homer. Good-bye and good luck. And thanks for all the adventures. Say hi to Sinbad for me!"

"I will tell Sinbad that you convey most humble regards to his glorious personage." The genie bowed. "And please give mine to Maddy and Jerome. Good-bye, Will, my friend. May you and your family prosper all the days of your lives." He touched his palms together and lifted them up to heaven, and he was gone. A pale green shimmer curled outward to the corners of the room and rolled away.

Will heard wheels swishing through the grass under his window. "Hey, Will!" Jerome called softly. Will sniffled, reached for a tissue, and blew his nose before pulling up the venetian blind.

"What are you *doing* here?" Will whispered.

"I have an idea for a magic adventure tomorrow. Let me in! Bugs are eating me alive!" Jerome said. Will raised the window and watched Jerome scramble through it and onto his bed.

"Why didn't you call?" Will asked.

Jerome crossed his arms. "What? And wake everybody up?"

"Anyway, listen, Jerome," Will said. "Homer is gone."

"Where'd he go?" Jerome turned around with his mouth open.

"He went home, to the place he came from. I was his last master, and he granted my heart's truest wish. He's free now."

"Homer's *free*? Why, because he saved your parents' diner?"

Will couldn't put it into words. "That, plus everything else good that happened."

"What'll he do now?" Jerome asked.

Will tried to remember what Homer had told him. "He's going to find his wife, and then they'll look for an oasis and sit in it and read books together." He thought of Homer and Mrs. Homer resting under a palm tree, reading stories aloud to each other, and he smiled. "They're going to live happily ever after, I guess. He *is* a book genie. Oh, and he sends his humble regards to your glorious personage."

Jerome shrugged and grinned.

"So what was the magic adventure?" Will asked.

"Well, it won't be magic now. But so what? Let's do something else," Jerome said. His eyes got the Look. "I know! I always wanted to try skateboarding down the path to the beach. I bet we'd really go shooting over those rocks. If it's high tide, we'd smack right into the water!"

"Let's talk about it tomorrow," Will suggested, leading Jerome toward the window.

"Okay. 'Night, Will!" Jerome said.

"Good night." He watched his cousin climb through the window and hop onto his skateboard. As he pulled the curtains closed, he could hear the sound of Jerome's skateboard rattling up the street.

Will reached for the light switch, then saw *The Arabian Nights* still lying open on the bed. He gently closed the book, placed it in the bookshelf, and turned out the light.

The End